READ ALOUD
COWBOY AND
INDIAN STORIES

Compiled by OSCAR WEIGLE
Illustrated by WILLIAM WIESNER

WONDER BOOKS • NEW YORK

ACKNOWLEDGMENTS

For the privilege of reprinting the material indicated, grateful acknowledgment and thanks are extended to the following sources:

CHILD LIFE Magazine—"Joey-Ha-Ha's Surprise," by Vivian Holgerson, copyright 1954. Reprinted by permission of the publisher.

Also the following, copyright by Wonder Books, Inc.: Come Visit My Ranch," copyright 1950; "The Story of Buffalo Bill," copyright 1954.

CONTENTS

Note to Parents

One of the most gratifying ways of bringing the precious feeling of closeness to your family is sharing the joys of reading with your children. More and more parents are discovering the pleasures of a daily Storytime Hour . . . a time for reading aloud to young children, helping them develop a lifetime love of books, stimulating their imagination, enriching their vocabularies, and teaching them fascinating facts about the world around them.

Read-Aloud books are especially planned for the small child who loves to listen to a story—and also for the beginning reader who is proud of his new talent and wants to show it off for your approval.

You will enjoy reading these stories to your young children. You will enjoy them perhaps even more when your child proudly reads the stories to you.

COME VISIT MY RANCH

by BALDWIN HAWES

BILLY lived on a ranch, and he had a horse of his own. Billy and his horse had a lot of fun together, but sometimes Billy was lonesome, because there were no other children for him to play with.

One day Billy wrote a letter to his cousins in the city.

"Dear Jack and Susan," he wrote. "If you would come and visit me on my ranch, we could have lots of fun together. Why don't you ask your mother and father to bring you for a visit soon? Billy."

Jack and Susan ran to show their mother and father Billy's letter.

"Why, isn't that nice of Billy!" said their mother.

"It certainly is," said their father. "I'll write a letter to Billy's father tomorrow. It would be fun to visit Billy on the ranch."

A few days later Jack and Susan, and their mother and father, boarded a big train that roared across the country, through the mountains—and deep into the ranch country where Billy lived.

Billy and his father met Jack and Susan, and their mother and father, at the station and drove them to the ranch in a station wagon. By the time they arrived at the ranch, it was late and they all went right to bed.

Next morning it was still dark when Billy woke Susan and Jack. He brought them each a pair of blue denim trousers which he called "levis."

He also brought them each a pair of high-heeled boots called "jack-boots."

Jack and Susan put on their levis, which fitted very tightly around the legs. They put on their jack-boots, which were hard to walk in, because they had such high heels.

Last of all, Billy gave them each a "ten-gallon" hat, just like the hats grown-up cowboys wear.

After breakfast, Billy said, "Let's go and see if Pete is breaking horses this morning."

"How can Pete break a horse?" asked Jack, puzzled.

"You'll see," said Billy, laughing.

When they reached the horse-breaking corral, Pete the cowboy was teaching a colt to wear a halter and to follow him when he pulled on the halter rope.

Jack and Susan and Billy climbed up on the top rail of the corral fence to watch.

"The colt is going to learn to wear a saddle and do whatever the rider wants him to do," Billy explained. "Pete is teaching him. Cowboys call this 'breaking' a horse. It usually takes about six weeks."

When the colt had had enough schooling for one day, Pete turned him loose and roped a big gray horse.

But he had never been ridden before, and he was startled when Pete put his foot in the stirrup and swung slowly into the saddle. The gray horse kicked out with his hind legs, but Pete stayed in the saddle. The horse rolled his eyes and kicked harder, but he could not shake Pete off his back.

He heard Pete talking softly to him, but now the horse was angry and wild. He leaped and bucked and plunged and twisted. He did everything he could think of to get Pete off his back, but Pete was a good rider and could outguess the horse.

Finally the horse quieted down. He was still angry, but he was tired out. Pete slid out of the saddle and took it off the horse's back. He stroked his neck and said, "One of these days, you'll be a fine cow horse."

"Let's go get some horses, and ride out to the west section to watch the branding," Billy suggested.

"Oh, boy!" Jack yelled. "Let's go!"

"What's branding?" asked Susan.

"We have to mark all our cattle so that everyone will know they belong to our ranch," Billy said. "Our brand looks like this," he added, kneeling down and drawing a design in the dirt with a stick.

Billy, Jack and Susan walked over to another corral. When Billy's horse saw him coming, he neighed and put his head through the bars to nuzzle Billy's hand. The other horses pricked up their ears and stared at Jack and Susan. Billy got saddles and bridles from the stable.

"Pick out the horses you want," he told Jack and Susan, "and I'll help you saddle them."

Susan chose a brown-and-white spotted horse, and Jack picked out a gray horse.

Billy's father joined them, and as they rode, Billy tried to teach Jack and Susan how to throw their ropes. He made a big loop of his own rope and whirled it slowly round and round his head. Then he started his horse at a gallop toward a small bush.

As he went past, he threw the loop over the bush. The loop tightened around the bush and pulled it from the ground. Susan and Jack tried to do it too, but it was very hard. They practiced and practiced.

At last they came to the branding fire. There were cowboys around it, some of them on horseback. Off to one side were the calves that were to be branded.

As Susan, Jack, Billy and his father rode up, a calf darted out of the herd. A cowboy on horseback galloped after it, swinging the loop of his lasso. He threw the loop, and as it settled around the calf's neck, the cow horse stopped short and braced his legs.

The cowboy swung out of the saddle and ran toward the calf, which was tugging to get free of the rope. The other end of the rope was tied to the saddle horn, and the well-trained cow horse was backing away so that the rope would stay tight.

When the cowboy reached the calf, another cowboy ran over to help him throw the calf to the ground. While they held it there, a third cowboy took a branding iron from the fire and quickly branded the calf. Then they let the calf go, and it ran back to the herd, bawling with fright, but not really hurt at all.

The cowboy who had roped the calf slapped the dust out of his clothes and coiled his rope. As he swung back into his saddle he patted his horse, and they rode off to find another calf that had to be branded.

"My, but cow horses have to know a lot of things!" said Susan.

"They sure do," said Billy. "Why, they have to know almost as much as the cowboys."

After a while Billy grew tired of watching the branding.

"I bet I can ride one of those calves," he said.

"I bet I can, too," said Jack.

"Well then, I bet I can, too," said Susan.

"You'll have to catch one first," cried Billy, sliding out of his saddle.

Billy told Jack and Susan that the best way to catch a calf was to walk up to the calf very slowly, pretending that you weren't interested in it at all, until you were close enough to jump on the calf's back. The children tried this, but usually the calves skittered off before they were close enough.

Then they tried chasing the calves, and Billy caught one by the tail.

Suddenly Susan cried, "I've got one! Oh, I've got one!" She was clinging to the calf's neck with both arms and the calf was running off as fast as it could go. Jack and Billy ran after them. After the calf had run a little way, it stopped and began to buck.

Susan cried, "Oooooh!" every time the calf bucked, but she hung on till the little calf bucked so hard that she slid right over its head and landed in a heap on the ground.

The calf ran off, and Billy and Jack helped Susan up.

"That was good riding," said Billy.

When they got back to the ranch, Billy's mother said that they were going to have a barbecue the next day.

Next morning, the first thing the three children did was to run over to the barbecue pit. The fire was still burning, but there was nothing left of the big pile of wood they had gathered the evening before. The meat was now a rich golden brown. It looked so very good that they could hardly wait for noon to come.

At last it was dinnertime! Everyone gathered around for the delicious barbecue —Billy and Susan and Jack, Billy's mother and father, Jack and Susan's mother and father, and all the cowboys on the ranch. In no time at all there was only one barbecued pig left!

When Jack and Susan's visit finally ended, they had had such a wonderful time that they hated to leave.

"Come visit my ranch again next summer!" shouted Billy, as he and the cowboys waved good-by.

THE STORY OF BUFFALO BILL

by JEFFREY COE

THERE was once a man named William Frederick Cody. Everyone called him Buffalo Bill. It was Buffalo Bill who gave American boys and girls a new game, the game they play perhaps more often than any other—"Cowboys and Indians."

Buffalo Bill also gave America the Wild West Show and the Rodeo. He gave the people of the whole country an unforgettable picture of the "great West that used to be." He was the last of the plainsmen, the last of the frontier scouts and the last of the great Indian fighters.

BILL CODY MEETS HIS FIRST INDIAN

Young Bill Cody was only eight years old when he saw his first Indian.

With his father and a guide, Bill had gone on a trip out into the great plains of Kansas.

Mr. Cody was looking for a good place to build a new home for his family.

It was early morning. The two men had ridden away to search for game. Bill was alone in the camp, lying asleep beside the campfire. Suddenly he was awakened by a strange noise.

Opening his eyes, Bill saw a tall, brown-skinned Indian, with feathers in his hair and a tomahawk in his belt. He was about to mount Bill's pony. The Indian's own pony, so thin and weak that it could hardly hold up its head, was standing miserably nearby.

Bill didn't know then that some day his name would be famous all over the world as the greatest Indian fighter of all time. All he knew was that he was alone in the camp with an unfriendly Indian, and that he was a frightened boy.

But Bill was also a brave boy. Without a moment's hesitation he jumped up, grabbed his rifle and aimed it at the Indian.

"What are you doing with my horse?" he said, trying hard to sound like a grown man.

"Me swap horses with paleface boy," the Indian replied.

"Oh, no, you won't!" Bill said firmly. He

cocked the rifle which was still pointed straight at the Indian. The hammer made a loud clicking sound in the still morning air.

"Paleface horse no good," the Indian said.

"He's good enough for me," said Bill. "So climb up on your old bag of bones and dust out of here."

The Indian stood by Bill's pony and said nothing. Several seconds passed in silence. Each second seemed like a year to the boy holding the rifle.

Bill spoke first. "I'll give you till I count three to get on your horse and git. Then I'll pull this trigger." He looked the Indian straight in the eye. "One..."

The Indian stood still.

"...two..."

The Indian hesitated. Then with a shrug he leaped to the back of his rickety horse and slowly rode away.

Bill watched him until he dropped out of sight over the hill. Not until then did Bill lower his gun. And not until then did he notice that his hands were shaking.

Suddenly, Bill remembered something that made his hands shake even harder. He remembered that the rifle wasn't loaded!

THE DANGEROUS WEST

The Indian had been driven slowly westward by the white man. The Great Plains were his last shelter, and the buffalo was his life. Buffalo meat was his food. The buffalo's skin provided his tents, his clothes, his moccasins, and the strings for his bows. The buffalo's bones gave him his needles, his knives and other crude tools he used in his daily life.

And now the white men were at last invading the Great Plains. Their prairie schooners rumbled across the land in ever larger numbers. They hunted the buffalo for meat and hides. They built homesteads, and plowed up fields and fed big herds of cattle on the tall grass. And slowly the buffalo herds drifted farther and farther west.

The Indians knew that slowly, mile by mile, the white men were destroying their hunting grounds. So it was only natural that every Indian thought of every white man as his enemy. In the Indian's mind it was perfectly right to take any paleface scalp he could get.

For this reason, a white man in the West lived in danger. He had to save his own life, from day to day, by being more quick-witted, braver and faster with a gun than his enemies.

That is why Bill Cody had been able to shoot ever since he was big enough to hold a gun, and why he had learned to ride a horse almost as soon as he could walk.

THE WILD STALLION HUNT

Once in a while, a white man and an Indian did make friends. Once Bill's father had done a good turn to an Indian brave. After that the Indian remained friendly to the Codys.

It was this brave who had given young Bill his favorite horse—a spotted Indian pony. The boy named his pony Prince. He helped to break him to the saddle, and rode him like a born horseman.

Bill had a cousin, Horace Billings, who was a famous herdsman and an expert with the lasso. One morning in early summer Horace came riding up to the Cody's front gate.

"Bill," he said, after he had slid down from the saddle and stretched his long legs. "I'm going on a horse hunt. How'd you like to come with me?"

"Yippee-yi-yi-yi!" yelled Bill, in a good imitation of an Indian war whoop. "Just wait'll I saddle up Prince!" He dashed off for the barn.

Bill's father came out of the house. "What's all this about a horse hunt?" he asked.

"Well, sir," Horace answered, "some cavalry horses got loose over at Fort Leavenworth. They think maybe a bunch of Indians stampeded 'em. Anyway, the Government's paying ten dollars a head for every one I can bring back. I'd sort of like to take Billy with me to look for 'em."

"But isn't Bill a little young for horse hunting?" Mr. Cody asked. "After all, he's only ten."

"I know," Horace replied. "But he's as good a rider and roper as most any man twice his age. And at ten dollars a head," he added, "likely he'll make himself some money."

At this point, Bill came galloping from the barn and pulled Prince up in a cloud of prairie dust. "Come on, Horace!" he cried. "Come on! Let's go horse hunting!"

Horace glanced at his uncle.

"All right, boys," Mr. Cody said. "Bill,

remember to keep a loose knot in your lasso!"

Late that afternoon, riding across the low, rolling hills and valleys of the prairie, Bill spied a band of wild horses grazing on a stand of buffalo grass. The leader of the band was a small, shaggy stallion. He was trotting back and forth in front of the herd. When the hunters came near, the wild stallion turned to face them; his front legs spread wide apart. He neighed wildly.

"I'll bet those army horses are somewhere near that wild bunch," Bill said.

"That's so," Horace agreed. "As a rule, runaway horses will stay as close to a wild bunch as they can. If we can just catch that little wild stallion, I think maybe we can round up the army stock. And we can probably take the rest of the wild bunch back to Leavenworth with them, too."

Horace shook out the loop in his rawhide lasso. "Here goes, Bill!" he said. "I'm going in after him. You follow me and get him if I miss."

Horace signaled his horse to gallop, and started toward the wild stallion.

The little wild horse wheeled sharply and

set off at a dead run. Horace's pony thundered at his heels. And behind Horace came Bill Cody. The reins lay loosely over Prince's neck as the boy made a loop in his lasso.

Horace threw his rope. The loop hung for a moment in the air. Just as it was about to settle over the wild stallion's neck, he swerved his body to one side. Horace's lasso slid down his flanks and crumpled to the ground.

Now it was Bill's turn. He came abreast

of the wild horse and cast his loop. The raw-hide rope wrapped itself around the wild horse's neck and tightened. Bill slid Prince to a quick stop. The stallion tumbled to the ground.

By this time Horace had recovered his lasso. Racing up, he circled it over the stallion's wildly kicking heels. Between the two ropers, the wild horse was helpless.

It was the next morning when the two horse hunters rode through the gates of Fort Leavenworth. Bill and Horace had the wild stallion between them, firmly roped by their lassos. And before them they drove the lost herd of army horses, plus about thirty of the wild bunch.

"Here are your horses," Horace said to the commander of the army post. "And a few more for your men to break, besides. And count 'em kind of careful, sir, because they'll cost you ten dollars apiece."

"But what about the wild stallion you two boys are holding on your ropes?" the officer asked. "Aren't you going to sell him, too?"

"Sir," said Horace, "young Bill Cody lassoed that horse himself. I think he should keep him!"

A PLEDGE TO REMEMBER

By the time Bill Cody was eleven years old his father had died. The boy was supporting his family now, and had very little chance to go to school. But he did attend the small, one-room schoolhouse a few miles from his home long enough to learn to read and write.

There was a company, called Russell, Majors and Waddell, that hauled freight between St. Joseph, Missouri, and San Francisco, California. Bill applied to them for a job.

Mr. Russell had known Bill's father and he wanted to do everything he could to help. But Bill was so very young that he hesitated about putting him to work.

"What can a boy of your age do?" he asked.

"I can ride, shoot, and herd cattle, sir," Bill replied. "But I'd rather be an extra on one of your bull trains."

"That's a man's work," said Mr. Russell. "And it's dangerous besides. But I'll let you try it for one trip. The pay is forty dollars a month."

This sum sounded like a small fortune. "You'll see that I can work like a man, sir," said Bill confidently. And he signed the company pledge.

The pledge that Bill Cody had to sign before he could go to work for Russell, Majors and Waddell is one that everyone today would do well to keep. It read: "I, William F. Cody, do hereby solemnly swear, before the great and living God, that while I am in the employ of Russell, Majors & Waddell, I will, under no circumstances, use profane language; that I will not quarrel or fight with any other employee of the firm and that in every respect I will conduct myself honestly, be faithful to my duties, and so direct all my acts as to win the confidence of my employers. So help me God!"

INDIAN ATTACK ON A BULL TRAIN

A bull train was made up of twenty or thirty wagons hauled by several yoke of oxen. The driver of each wagon was called a bull-whacker. He walked beside the wagon and carried a long whip. This he cracked over the oxen's heads to keep them moving as quickly as they can move.

The wagons themselves looked like ordinary prairie schooners, except that they were bigger and stronger. They were protected from the weather by a double covering of tough canvas. Each wagon was able to carry more than three tons of freight.

Besides the bull-whackers, there were cattle drivers and "extra" hands who did odd jobs. As an extra, Bill Cody's job was to ride up and down the train delivering orders from the wagon master to the various bull-whackers. This was a job that Bill enjoyed.

When nightfall came, the wagons of the train formed themselves into a big circle as protection against the Indians. In the center of the circle, the trainmen built a large campfire over which they cooked their evening meal. Then, as the western stars came out and the pale moon spread its dim light over the prairie, the hands played their banjos and sang the old songs of the frontier.

But life on a bull train was hard work, and soon every man was curled up in his blanket beside the fire. Every man, that is, except the guards who were posted all around the camp to keep watch against the redskins.

It was on his first trip with a bull train that Bill Cody shot his first Indian.

One evening, as the trainmen were eating

their dinner, shots suddenly rang out in the quiet air. The men ran for their rifles and crawled under the wagons. Bill Cody rested his rifle across the wagon's tongue. Then he peered out and saw more than two hundred Indians riding in a circle around the wagons. They were firing their guns and arrows into the wagon train.

Frank McCarthy, who was the boss of the train, called his men together.

"It looks to me, boys," he said, "like we're outnumbered about ten to one. And more Injuns are comin' up every minute. I figure we'd better skedaddle out of here and try to make it back to Fort Kearny."

As quietly as they could, the men left the wagon train and retreated down between the high banks of a dry creek. Fort Kearny was twenty miles away.

All night the men plodded along, keeping alert against the Indians who, they knew, were sure to follow.

After they had walked several hours, Bill fell a few yards behind. After all, he was a boy trying his best to do a man's work.

Suddenly, just ahead of him, Bill saw the head and shoulders of a war-painted Indian

rise up over the edge of the creek's bank.
The Indian slowly brought a rifle to his
shoulder and took careful aim at one of Bill's
companions who was walking up ahead.
Without thinking twice, Bill raised his own
rifle and fired. The Indian tumbled off the
bank into the creek bed and lay still.

At the sound of the shot, the other trainmen ran back to see what had happened.
When they saw the dead Indian, they
cheered and crowded around Bill, clapping
him on the back. Frank McCarthy put an
arm around Bill's shoulder and said, "Well,
boys, little Bill Cody has killed himself an
Injun, and he's done it like a man."

Bill Cody felt mighty proud, and also
mighty grown-up.

THE PONY EXPRESS

Bill worked on and off for Russell, Majors and Waddell for three more years. In between bull train trips, he went to classes in the little one-room schoolhouse. Then something happened that changed his whole life.

Mr. Russell had decided to set up a fast mail service across the continent from St. Joseph to California. By stagecoach, the trip took several weeks, by bull train more than two months. Mr. Russell figured that, with crack riders mounted on swift ponies, the journey could be done in nine days.

So he hired the finest riders in the West and mounted them on the fastest ponies he could buy. They carried the mail at a dead run over the entire two-thousand-mile route.

There was a relay station every fifteen miles along the way. At every station, the rider changed ponies. Each rider rode fifteen miles on his first pony, fifteen miles on the second, fifteen miles on the third and so on, until he came to the end of his route. Then he began his return trip back to his home base.

The mail was carried in saddlebags, and each rider's load was limited to twenty pounds. In order to get as much mail as possible in the twenty-pound limit, Pony Express letters were written on tissue paper, just as many air mail letters are today.

Bill Cody heard that Pony Express riders were to be paid one hundred and twenty-five dollars a month. This would allow him to support his family in style. So he went once more to see Mr. Russell.

And once more, Mr. Russell said, "Bill, I'm afraid you're too young to ride the Express."

"I'm fourteen, sir," replied Bill. "And I've been doing my job on the bull trains."

"That's so," Mr. Russell had to agree. "But riding the Pony Express is different. You'll be all by yourself in dangerous Indian country. You'll have to ride harder and faster than any man ever rode before. And you'll have to do it every day in the week. It'll be tough, Bill."

"I know that, sir," Bill answered. "But I'm

tough, too. I can ride with the best of 'em and I can shoot with the best of 'em. And I sure do need the job."

Mr. Russell smiled. "You win, son. I've been watching you and I've been proud of you. Starting tomorrow, you're riding the Pony Express."

Bill enjoyed riding the Pony Express more than he had ever enjoyed anything in his life. Every minute of the time he had to be on the alert. For it was well-known that large sums of money were sometimes carried in the Pony Express mailbags. The riders had to be on the watch every minute for bandits as well as Indians.

Bill carried a revolver in a holster on his belt and a rifle in a scabbard slung to his saddle.

One day, Bill was riding through a narrow, rocky ravine. Suddenly a white man, with a bandanna tied across the lower part of his face, leaped out in front of him. The man had a rifle pointed squarely at the middle of Bill's stomach.

Bill realized that the outlaw had the drop on him. There was nothing to do but bring his horse to a stop.

"All right, sonny," the outlaw said flatly. "I know you've got money in that mail pouch. I don't want to hurt you if I don't have to. So you just slide down off that pony and give me your saddlebag. Then you can scoot on along like nothing happened."

The man stepped up to Bill's pony and reached for the bridle.

Bill touched his pony's flanks as a signal. Then he leaned back in the saddle and pulled on the reins. The pony reared up on his hind legs, his forelegs fanning the air. One hoof struck the outlaw on the head and knocked him out.

Bill got off his pony and quickly tied the man up hand and foot. Then he began to look for the bandit's horse which he knew must be somewhere in the nearby bushes and rocks. By the time Bill found the horse, the outlaw had come to. Bill untied his legs, forced him to mount the horse and then tied his legs together again under the horse's belly. Leading the outlaw's horse, Bill brought his prisoner to the next relay station.

The Pony Express was late that day, but Bill Cody was a hero.

INJUNS ON THE WARPATH

Young as he was, Bill Cody's fame as a rider and a scout had spread all over the West. Cattlemen and bull-whackers told stories about him as they sat around their campfires at night. And one of the stories went like this:

One morning, as Bill was starting out on his regular ride, the station boss warned him to be on the lookout for trouble.

"Injuns are on the warpath all around here," he said. "Be sure to keep your eyes skinned."

Bill promised to watch carefully and galloped away, leaving a cloud of prairie dust.

Several miles from the station, riding

through a small canyon, Bill saw the feathered headdress of an Indian sticking up over the top of a pile of rocks. He signaled his pony and put on a burst of speed. He lay forward along the pony's neck in order to become the smallest possible target for the Indians' guns. It was well that he did. At that instant he heard the crack of a shot and the buzz of a rifle ball as it whizzed over his head.

Out from behind the rocks came a party of Indians, mounted on pinto ponies. Filling the air with screeching war cries, they set out to run Bill down.

Bill knew he was riding for his life. Looking back over his shoulder, he saw that the Indians in the lead carried no rifles. They were armed only with bows and arrows. Bill slowed his pony just enough to let them get within range of his revolver. Firing behind him as he raced along, he shot them out of their homemade saddles one by one. After two or three of the leading redskins had fallen, the others gave up the chase.

When Bill finally brought his tired horse into the next relay station, he discovered that it had two Indian arrows in its sides.

CIVIL WAR SCOUT

Every day that he rode the Pony Express was an exciting adventure for Bill. But in time, telegraph wires were being strung across the continent. The brave day of the Pony Express was drawing to a close.

The Civil War was raging between the states, and young Bill Cody wanted to enlist in the Union Army. He had to wait until he was old enough. But when he did enlist, he was immediately assigned to duty as a scout —his reputation as a frontiersman had preceded him into the Army. He served as a scout, mostly in the western campaigns, throughout the rest of the war.

BILL CODY—BUFFALO HUNTER

It was after the Civil War was over that William Frederick Cody got the name of Buffalo Bill.

The railroad was now being built across

the plains. The twelve hundred men who were employed in the track-laying gang of the Kansas Pacific Railroad required a lot of food. Buffalo still were plentiful and the railroad wanted to hire hunters to kill fresh meat to feed the workers.

The railroad people knew that Bill was an experienced frontiersman who could be trusted with any job. So the foreman of the Kansas Pacific track gang went to see him.

"Bill," he said, "if you can kill us twelve buffalo a day, six days a week, we'll pay you five hundred dollars a month. Think you can do it?"

"Just give me a wagon and a driver to haul in the meat," Bill replied, "and you've got a deal."

Bill had a horse named Brigham that he had trained especially to hunt buffalo. Brigham knew his job perfectly. In the midst of a herd of buffalo, Bill didn't have to touch the bridle. Brigham made the right moves almost by instinct.

Bright and early the next morning, Bill reported to the foreman. "I'm ready to go to work," he said. "Where's your meat wagon and driver?"

"We can't send a wagon out with you until you've shot some buffalo," the foreman told Bill. "You go shoot 'em and then we'll come out and get 'em."

"I've got a better idea than that," Bill replied. And, wheeling Brigham around, he dashed off across the plain.

About a mile from the camp, Bill found a herd of twenty or twenty-five buffalo. He rode around them, waving his hat, firing his gun into the air and yelling as loudly as he could. At last, the buffalo stampeded toward the railroad camp.

When the stampeding herd came within a few hundred yards of the camp, Bill brought Brigham alongside a big buffalo bull and dropped him with a shot in the shoulder. As the buffalo fell, Brigham side-stepped his falling body and closed up to the next one. Bill fired again and killed the next buffalo just as quickly. One after another, Bill killed twelve buffalo. The last one fell amost inside the camp itself.

The railroad boss was furious. "What do you mean, Cody," he yelled, "by bringing those critters this close to camp? They might have stampeded all over us!"

"You wouldn't give me a wagon to haul 'em in," Bill replied, "so I thought I'd better let 'em furnish their own transportation."

After that, a meat wagon went out with Bill every day. And it always came back full.

Before his job with the railroad was finished, Bill had become even more famous as a buffalo hunter than he had been as a scout and Indian fighter. It wasn't long before all his friends were calling him Buffalo Bill.

There was a man by the name of Bill Comstock who was the Army chief of scouts at nearby Fort Wallace. When he heard that Bill Cody was being called Buffalo Bill, he rode over to the railroad camp and looked Bill up.

"Cody," he said, "I figure I'm a sight better man with a buffalo gun than you will ever be. If there's going to be a Buffalo Bill, I claim it ought to be Buffalo Bill Comstock, not Buffalo Bill Cody. What do you say to that?"

"I say let's have a shooting match and see," Bill answered.

So a contest between the two hunters was arranged. A crowd of several hundred people —plainsmen, scouts, soldiers and railroad workers—came to watch the sport.

When everything was ready, the two hunters mounted their horses and set off.

As the first buffalo herd was sighted, both men dashed to the attack. Riding in among

the wildly running beasts, they shot as fast
as they could load and fire their guns. Bill
didn't have to worry about guiding Brigham.
As soon as Bill fired at one buffalo, Brigham
moved into the correct position for the next
shot.

By the time the last buffalo was down, the
hunters had ridden for miles, and carcasses
were strung out all over the prairie.

The hunters stopped to give their horses
a rest and eat a bite of lunch while the
referees added up each man's total. They
found that in the first trial, Bill had shot
thirty-eight animals and Comstock had shot
twenty-three.

"Just wait till the afternoon's over," Comstock said good-naturedly. "It will be a different story."

Bill grinned. "Maybe so. We'll see," he said.

Lunch was hardly over when a second, but smaller, herd was sighted. The contestants leaped into their saddles and went after them. This time, Bill got eighteen and Comstock fourteen.

Within a few minutes a third herd came into view. Bill hurriedly rode Brigham into the milling herd. The marvelous horse did his part of the job perfectly. And again Bill's kill was greater than Comstock's. This ended the contest.

When the referees added up the score, the final total was sixty-nine buffalo for Bill Cody and forty-eight for Bill Comstock.

"I guess I know when I'm licked," Comstock said. He held out his hand. "I'm mighty glad to know you, Buffalo Bill."

Buffalo Bill Cody laughed as they shook hands. "I'll tell you my secret," he said. "It's Brigham. This horse knows more about buffalo than any two-legged hunter I've ever seen in my life."

BUFFALO BILL'S WILD WEST SHOW

On many occasions Bill had traveled to the eastern states. It always made him unhappy to see how little most Easterners knew about the great West that Bill loved so well.

"If the Easterners won't come out here to see the West," he once said to a friend, "I'd like to take the West to them."

"That might be quite a job," his friend replied.

"Yes, it might be," Bill agreed. "But, by golly, I may do it some day at that!"

Bill's chance came a few years later. The people of Omaha, Nebraska, decided to have a Frontier Day celebration. Their idea was to put on a big show that would represent the real West. Everyone agreed that Buffalo Bill Cody was the man to put the show together.

Bill was delighted to tackle the job. He

immediately sent messages to all his old friends of the frontier, asking for their help.

Into Omaha came streaming herds of buffalo which had been rounded up on the plains. Longhorn cattle from the western ranches. Friendly Indians from the reservations. Cowboys, plainsmen, soldiers from the frontier forts. Prairie schooners, bull trains and even the famous old Deadwood Stagecoach that Bill had once driven.

When Bill put them all together, he had the most colorful and exciting show the world had ever seen.

Bill's show made such a big hit with the people of Omaha that it gave him the greatest idea of his life.

"Now I can let people in the East see what the West is really like," he decided. "We'll keep our show together and take it to every city in America."

And that is what he did. It was not many years before people in all sections of the country—and even in Europe and parts of Asia—were flocking by the thousands to see Buffalo Bill's Wild West Show.

And what a thrilling sight it was to see! Indian braves by the hundreds, all dressed in war paint and feathers, rode their tough little ponies furiously around the ring, filling the air with blood-chilling war whoops. Cowboys herded great droves of cattle and rode bucking broncos and did fancy rope tricks. Soldiers from crack cavalry regiments went through their mounted drills at a dead run. The greatest marksmen in the West showed off their fancy shooting tricks.

Bill himself, dressed in white buckskins and mounted on a tall white horse, opened the show. Later in the performance he gave his own special exhibition of trick riding and trick shooting.

One of the most exciting parts of the show was the Indian chase of the Deadwood Stagecoach. The coach first entered the arena at a run, filled to overflowing with passengers. After it came a band of Indians, whooping and shooting into the air. Then the Indians rode howling around the coach, fighting a running gun-battle with the passengers inside and on top. Just when it looked as if all the people in the coach would be killed, they were saved by a rescue party of U. S. Cavalrymen who dashed onto the scene and defeated the Indians.

No boy or girl who ever saw this make-believe battle was likely to forget it in a hurry.

All in all, it was a grand and glorious show. And as the years went by, Bill heard audiences shout and cheer in dozens of different languages.

Bill traveled with his Wild West Show until he was an old man. Then, full of honors and with his name known all around the world, he retired at last for a well-earned rest to his ranch in the Rocky Mountains of Colorado.

But although Bill Cody no longer can be seen riding his spirited white horse, his name will be remembered for many years to come. He will be remembered not just as an Indian fighter and scout and buffalo hunter, nor as the man who took the West to every part of the civilized world.

He was all of these in his lifetime. But today he is even more.

Today Buffalo Bill is remembered as one of the great men of the Old West. His name is a symbol of courage and determination of the pioneers and frontiersmen who first rode over the broad plains and high mountains.

JOEY-HA-HA'S SURPRISE

by *VIVIAN HOLGERSON*

BIG Bill Bolder set out one fall day to stay with Joey-Ha-Ha, his Indian friend. But the nearer he came to Joey's cabin, the slower he moved. For Bill had remembered about the river!

The river was between Bill and the cabin. The only way Bill could reach the cabin was to swim across the river.

A mile downstream at the fishing hole,

the river was narrow and deep. Two miles downstream at Feather Falls, the river was narrow and swift. In front of the cabin, the river was deep and swift and wide! And in all these places, the water was wet and cold!

On hot summer days, it was nice to swim across in the cold water. On frosty winter days, it was fun to slide across on the thick, smooth ice. But in the spring and fall, the water was too cold for swimming and not cold enough for skating. So Bill sat down to think about how to get across. Pretty soon Joey came and found him there.

"Why you stop here? Why you not come home?" asked Joey.

"Maybe I won't come home," said Bill with a shiver. "That water's cold!"

"I got nice surprise. Make you feel warm," said Joey.

"Nothing would make me feel warm except crossing the river without getting wet. If I had a hatchet I'd make a raft," said Bill.

"Got no hatchet," Joey laughed.

"With a rope, I'd swing across."

"Got no rope," Joey laughed.

"If I had a horse, I could ride across."

"Got no horse." Joey laughed harder.

"If only there were a bridge," said Bill.

"Got no bridge. But got nice surprise," and Joey laughed so hard he rolled on the ground and almost choked.

"*Well!*" scowled Bill. And he turned his back and stared at the trees, feeling mighty cross with his friend for laughing.

The trees were all around him. They were big and tall and straight. They had thick, sturdy trunks. They had leafy, branching tops, and long, tough roots.

Suddenly Bill's eyes began to sparkle. He laughed and slapped his sides, and shouted "Whoopee!" Then he leaped to his feet, whizzed past Joey, and raced down the trail toward the river.

"Wait for me. See nice surprise," shouted Joey, running after Bill.

"Can't wait!" yelled Bill, and he kept right on going.

"Wait! Don't jump in river! See nice surprise!" yelled Joey.

But Bill didn't answer, for he had reached the river. But he didn't jump in. He turned to the right and ran downstream on the river bank.

"Too bad. He not see nice surprise," said

Joey. And he climbed into a pretty birch-bark canoe and paddled slowly down the river after Bill.

But Bill kept right on running downstream as hard as he could. For Bill had thought of a way to make a good bridge.

He was going to use a great big tree for his bridge. It grew on the river bank right across from the fishing hole. Each time Bill went fishing, he looked at the tree and wondered why it didn't fall down.

The roots of this tree no longer held it firmly into the earth. The thick trunk leaned out so far over the river that the leafy branches shaded the fishing hole very well.

"I'll cut a few roots and the trees will tumble down. It will make a fine bridge," said Bill. He dropped his rifle and his pack, pulled out his hunting knife and began to cut and slash at the tough roots.

The roots snapped and the earth crumbled. The tree began to creak and groan and shiver and shake. Then the roots bounced out of the earth and knocked the knife out of Bill's hand. He tumbled over backward into the bushes. With a thundering *crack* and a mighty *swoosh*, the tree fell.

For several minutes the air was filled with flying twigs and leaves and branches and rocks. Water splashed. Birds squawked. Squirrels fled for cover. And the tree shook, shivered, and settled on the ground.

Then all grew quiet, and Big Bill Bolder crawled from the bushes and looked at the tree. The tangled roots lay near him on the south side of the river. The leafy branches lay on the north bank, just opposite. And in between, high and dry, stretched the thick, sturdy trunk!

Bill had a bridge.

"Joey-Ha-Ha!" yelled Bill, as he picked

up his rifle and pack. But Joey didn't answer. So, since Joey wasn't there to see his nice surprise, Bill leaped onto the bridge, and started to cross the river.

Halfway across, the tree jiggled. But Bill kept on going. Three-quarters of the way across, the tree jerked. But Bill kept on going. He didn't fall, but he did look back. And what he saw made him blink.

The earth under the roots was moving. The thick trunk was quivering and shaking. The tangled roots were sliding faster, faster, *faster* down toward the river!

"Joey-Ha-Ha!" yelled Big Bill Bolder, as the bridge slipped out from under his feet. And with a mighty leap toward dry land, Bill soared off into space!

As Big Bill Bolder leaped from his tree-bridge, the roots fell into the river with a mighty *splash*. Up in the air went a fountain of water. Up in the air went the thick, sturdy trunk. Up in the air went the leafy, branching top.

Then the roots were caught by the swift river current. Around swung the roots. Around swung the top—*right into the path of Big Bill Bolder!*

One second Bill was soaring through space as free as a bird. His outstretched arms had almost touched the firm, dry bank. Then he crashed headlong into the treetop!

"Help!" yelled Bill, as he sailed into the leafy darkness of the branches.

"Help!" yelled Bill, as he hurtled down toward the wet, cold water.

"Help!" yelled Bill, as the deerskin straps on his pack caught on a limb and stopped him with a jerk. As he dangled from the tree, safe and dry, Bill was as mad as a hornet.

He had no bridge. He had no surprise. He didn't even have Joey-Ha-Ha, his Indian friend, to help him.

But Joey had heard the mighty crash when the tree fell. He had reached the river bend in time to see the roots drop into the water. He had seen Bill sail into the branches of the tree. And in his birchbark canoe he raced to the rescue.

"Quick! Jump into the river!" shouted Joey, as he swept under the bobbing tree.

But Bill could not jump. The deerskin straps were holding him fast.

"Cut the straps!" shouted Joey.

But Bill couldn't cut the straps. He had lost his knife. And when Joey handed him his knife, Bill dropped it into the river!

"Slip your arms from the straps!" shouted Joey.

But Bill couldn't even do that. He struggled. He yanked. He tried to break the straps. But they were new and strong. At last Bill stopped struggling, and dangled on the limb, breathless and dizzy.

Then Bill heard a sound that Joey had been hearing for a long time. It was louder than the churn and swirl of the river. It was louder than the creak and rustle of the branches. It was the roar of the swift water sweeping over Feather Falls!

Now Big Bill Bolder was as brave as can be, but he certainly didn't want to shoot-the-chute over Feather Falls. He just had to free himself from the tree, and fast!

He tried again. This time he didn't yank and pull. This time Bill was wise. He used all his strength and pulled himself up onto the branch. Now, without his weight to tighten the straps, they fell loose and free. All he had to do now was to slip his arms out, and to jump into the river.

But Bill had waited too long. All the while the tree had been sweeping faster and faster down the river. As he started to free himself, the roots of the tree reached the edge of the Falls. The rush of the water lifted them into the air. The trunk and the branches sank deeper into the water, caught on a snag, and stopped moving.

The snag was not a very big one. It was not a very strong one. It held the tree for only a few seconds. But that was long enough for several things to happen.

The sudden jolt shook Bill. It swung the tree around. It pulled the roots away from the Falls and swept them against the rocks on the south side of the river.

Then the snag broke. The tree pulled loose and began to move. But the roots, slammed against the rocks, were wedged there. The swift current pulled the tree around in a half-circle. Around swung the trunk. Around swung Bill and Joey and the birchbark canoe, right toward the rocks on the north side of the river!

"*Snap*," went the limb that Bill held.

"*Swoosh*," went the limb, and Bill and Joey and the canoe sailed off into space!

"Joey-Ha-Ha!" yelled Bill, as he hit the ground and bounced into the bushes. Then he sat up and looked around.

Joey, shaken but unhurt, was crawling out of the bushes. Leaves, twigs and branches were scattered in every direction. And jiggling and trembling on the very edge of Feathers Falls was Bill's bridge.

But not for long. With an ear-splitting roar, the tree swept right over the foaming falls.

"Too bad. No more bridge," said Joey.

"And no more crossing the river without getting wet," moaned Bill.

"You not have to get wet. I make nice surprise, too," said Joey. And he pointed to the nice birchbark canoe lying upside down but unharmed on the river bank.

"A *canoe!*" yelled Big Bill Bolder. "Why, if I had listened to you, I wouldn't have needed to make that silly bridge!"

"Bridge not silly. You get across river. You not get wet," said Joey. And he laughed.

"Why, I *did* at that!" yelled Bill. And sitting there on the firm, dry land, he looked at the wet, cold water, and laughed and laughed and laughed.

AN INDIAN LULLABY

Rock-a-by, rock-a-by, little brown baby,
Safe in the branches so green and so high.
Shut your black eyes and go to sleep, baby,
While the wood-wind sings, "Hush-a-by-by."
"Hush-a-by-hush," 'tis the voice of the forest,
"Hush-a-by-hush," the leaves seem to say.
"Hush-a-by-hush," sing the wild birds in
    chorus
Up in the treetops so far, far away.
Rock-a-by, rock-a-by, swinging so gently,
See, from the dark woods, so cool and so
    deep,
The little gray squirrel, the timid brown
    rabbit,
Are coming to see if papoose is asleep.
Mother will watch by her little brown baby,
Swinging aloft on the green branch so high.
No harm can come to the little brown baby,
Hush-a-by, rock-a-by, hush-a-by-by.

THE LEGEND OF THE BEAR PAW JARS

by LaVERE ANDERSON

MANY *many* moons ago, in the land of the Santa Clara Pueblo Indians, there was great trouble.

The Santa Clara Indians lived in the American Southwest, in what is now the state of New Mexico. They were kind and friendly people, and happy until the trouble came.

Their trouble was that for a long time there had been no rain. The sky was like a hot blue bowl over their heads. The sun was like a round yellow fire. The prairie grass dried up. The flowers shriveled. The leaves on the trees hung straight down.

And all the people were so very thirsty.

The men were too thirsty to hunt buffalo for food.

The women were too thirsty to make the beautiful clay jars in which to keep the food.

The horses were too thirsty to run, the dogs too thirsty to bark.

And worst of all, the little children were too thirsty to play.

"We must have water. We cannot live without water," said the Chief of the Tribe. "But the streams have dried away. And there are no rain clouds in the sky." He was old and wise, but he did not know what to do.

"We must have water," agreed the braves. "Nothing can live without water. That is why all the wild animals have left our land. Even the prairie dogs have gone away to hunt water." The braves were young and strong, and they could shoot straight arrows, but they did not know what to do.

"We must have water," nodded the squaws. "Without water, our throats grow too dry to

swallow food. And without food we all grow
thin and weak." The squaws were good and
worked hard, but they did not know what to
do.

"Oh, yes, we *must* have water!" cried all
the little children. They had bright eyes and
they could run fast and jump high, but they
did not know what to do, either.

Days passed, and each day everybody went
out hunting water, but nobody could find
any.

They all grew thin and weak, while over
head the hot blue sky and the fiery yellow sun
blazed down.

At last, in all the village, only one brave
was left who still had a little strength. He
was a fine young brave and he loved his
people dearly.

He said, "I shall go out once more and try
to find water for my people, for without
water we cannot live."

Early the next morning he started.

All day he hunted.

He grew hot and tired and weak.

But he would not give up.

Then at last he saw a bear! A big, fat,
black bear! It was the first animal he had

een all day. And the bear did not look
hirsty! It looked strong. Its hair gleamed
hiny black in the sunlight.

"Oh, what a fine happy bear!" said the
rave.

Suddenly he thought: "That bear must
know where to get water! Else he would have
gone far away from this land like the other
animals. If I follow him, perhaps he will lead
ne to it."

The young brave began to follow the bear.

It was hard work, for the big black bear

was strong and could move fast. And the brave was growing very weak and could not move fast at all.

The brave had to be careful, too, that the bear did not see him.

Sometimes the bear got so far ahead he was lost from sight. Then the brave had to follow the animal's tracks in the dry dust.

But there was one good sign. The bear was going in the direction of the Indian village

At last the bear disappeared in a thicke of trees on the side of a small hill. The brave crept closer and peered through the bushes

To his joy, he saw that the bear was get ting a drink!

The big black bear had led him to a hidder spring in the side of the hill. It was really not very far from the village, but it was hidden in thick undergrowth, and it bubbled up and drained away so quickly that even the bear must have found it only by accident

The brave waited until the bear had drunk his fill and had gone lumbering off down the hillside.

Thankfully, then, the young brave stum bled on weak legs to the spring, fell on hi knees and drank the clear, cold water.

Then, feeling stronger, he jumped up and hurried to the village, shouting his good news.

"Water! Water! The black bear has led me to water, so that we may live!"

Almost unbelieving, the people listened to the happy words.

Then they gathered all the pots and jars and water jugs in camp—everyone, even the littlest children carried a jar—and they all followed the brave to the wonderful spring.

There they all drank of the clear water. They filled their jars and took the water to the village for the old people and babies, and the horses and the dogs.

For many more days it did not rain in the land of the Santa Clara Indians, but the people were not thirsty any more, for they had their spring.

And later, when the autumn rains came and the earth was washed fresh and clean again, and the ponds filled and the streams ran full, the Indians remembered the bear.

"We will show our thanks to him," they said.

From then on, whenever they made a new clay jar they put on it the print of a bear's paw, just like the track the young brave had followed in the dry dust that day.

That is why, even today, when you visit a museum where there is Santa Clara pottery, you will see big earthen jars and on them the print of a bear's paw.

And you will know that the print was put on the jars by the grateful Santa Clara Pueblo Indians in memory of the big black bear who saved their village.

LITTLE FOX WHO TREMBLED

by LAURON EDWARDS

LITTLE Fox came out of the pueblo, which was his home on the high, barren mesa, and looked up at the cloudless sky. He could feel the excitement in the village, for this was the day when the dances began.

"Oh, if I could only take part in the dances —or, best of all, beat the drum," Little Fox thought to himself.

"There will be no rain on Hopi corn today," said his grandmother, who was sitting near the doorway grinding corn upon the same stone that she had ground it on for all the years Little Fox could remember.

Little Fox knew that there would have to be rain or there would be no corn for the people in the Hopi Indian village. Without corn there would be no food.

Even so, Little Fox trembled. The great storms frightened him. The lightning flashed and the thunder made the earth shiver, so he always stayed close to his own pueblo.

Early in the spring Little Fox had helped plant corn in the sandy, barren ground of the mesa. His father had been using the family planting stick, but Little Fox had hunted for several hours until he found a piece of greasewood on the desert that was thick and tough. He had sharpened it until the stick would dig through the sand and into the good soil and moisture far below.

Into each hole Little Fox had dropped a few kernels of corn—beautiful corn, Little Fox thought, for it was many-colored. Some kernels were blue, others white, yellow, red or pale purple.

The corn had grown. The kernels that Little Fox planted came up as tall and green as any of the men's plantings, but now the hot winds blew day and night. No clouds came in the sky to offer the hope of rain.

"Grandmother, when the men dance will they carry a message to the rain gods and tell them we must have rain?" Little Fox asked the old woman.

"They must. They must," Grandmother murmured as she took another handful of corn and put it on the grinding stone.

Little Fox saw Black Cloud going toward the other dancers.

"May I beat a drum?" Little Fox called to him.

Black Cloud frowned. "How can a little fox who trembles at the voice of the rain god beat the drum for the dances that will bring the storm?"

"Bring me the *piki* stone, Little Fox, so I can make our dinner," Grandmother called to him.

Little Fox wanted to follow along with the men, but he obeyed his grandmother and went for the *piki* stone. It was an oblong stone, smooth and flat on top. Little Fox

remembered the day his father had brought the new stone home and he had helped rub oily seeds into it until the stone was smooth and glossy.

"Grandmother, may I make the bread?" Little Fox asked.

"No, you might drop it and we must not waste one little bit," his grandmother replied.

Little Fox said nothing. He had watched Grandmother make the bread so often. She took a thin mixture of the corn gruel in her hand and spread it over the hot *piki* stone. He knew he could do it and not spill one bit.

Little Fox wanted to ask if he could wait until one of the thin cakes was cooked and then quickly roll it up. It would take only a minute for it to cool and harden so that he could eat it. They were good and he was hungry.

Little Fox knew what Grandmother would say. They had so little corn, everyone had to wait and share together.

The Indian boy kicked at the dirt with his bare toes and walked through the village. The little burro chewing corn husks nearby looked up and blinked sleepily, but Little Fox didn't even give him a pat on the head.

"I cannot beat the drum. I cannot make bread. I tremble at the sound of the storm. I am not good for anything," Little Fox told himself.

He walked in the hot August sun until he came to a rocky ledge. In the distance he could see Corn Rock. Little Fox had heard the story of Corn Rock many times. Once it had been two gigantic ears of corn that had turned to stone. "If I could only turn it back into corn," Little Fox thought, "then the men would let me beat the drum." But he knew that was impossible.

Little Fox walked and walked along the mesa. He didn't watch where he was going or see how far he had come from the village. Suddenly, in the distance, he heard the drums begin. It was time for the dances and if he didn't hurry he would miss them.

Even now, Little Fox knew that the men were dancing and waving the feathers of the mighty eagle above their swaying heads. How Little Fox loved all the excitement, and he was missing it all!

Little Fox could hear the throbbing of the

chant across the land and he turned to run as fast as he could. But then, on the horizon, he saw great rain clouds. They grew darker and darker every second. Little Fox trembled. He did not want to be away from the village when the lightning flashed and the thunder shook the ground.

"I must run," he thought, but for a moment more he watched the gray clouds.

A wind began to blow and the clouds moved off to the south.

"No. This way! This way!" Little Fox cried out loudly. "Don't you hear the dancing and the chanting?"

The clouds seemed to hesitate and the wind blew less. The clouds moved closer above Little Fox's head.

"This way," he called.

The clouds drew nearer and nearer and pulled the sun behind them. They looked down on Little Fox and scowled. The lightning crashed not far off. Still Little Fox waited.

"I must show Rain Cloud the way," he told himself. "So often he becomes lost and then the rain falls on the rocks or skips over the corn fields.

"I'll lead you, great storm!" Little Fox cried through his trembling lips.

Crash! The thunder shook the mesa. The wind caught in Little Fox's black hair and the large wet drops pelted his face. He began to run, but not too fast. He ran just fast enough to keep the rain at his heels.

"Follow me! Follow me!" he cried.

Right through the fields he ran and into the village and past the dancers, with the rain behind him now—not angry rain, but light, laughing, steady rain.

"I thought this was Little Fox Who Trembled," Black Cloud cried as he lifted the boy into the air.

"I did tremble," Little Fox confessed, "but I knew the rain might become lost and I had to lead it. I will never tremble again."

"There will be a feast tonight," Black Cloud laughed, "for Little Fox, who is now Big Fox, has shown the rain god the way."

Little Fox was so happy he thought he might burst.

Then Black Cloud called, "Come, everyone, we will have another dance—and Little Fox, who is now Big Fox, will beat the drum for us!"

ALI ABU AND THE COWBOYS

by *BLANCHE BOSHINSKI*

"WHEW, it's hot!" Jimmy said as he stopped his horse and wiped his forehead with the back of his hand. "I'm thirsty."

Cowboy John pushed his big western hat back on his head and nodded. "Look at the heat waves rising off that sand and sagebrush out there on the prairie."

Jimmy squinted his eyes against the hot sun. "It looks like water out there," he pointed excitedly.

"Just a mirage—it only *looks* like water," Cowboy John laughed. "Like the mirages that people see on deserts."

"Deserts!" Jimmy exclaimed. "We should have camels out here on the prairie. *They* don't need much water."

Cowboy John nodded his head. "That's what some folks thought once. There's a stream over here beyond that ridge. We'll water the horses and I'll tell you about a camel that once came to the United States."

Cowboy John and Jimmy tied their horses near the cool stream that flowed from the rocks and settled themselves under a huge old cottonwood tree.

"It was about a hundred years ago that the United States Government brought camels to this country," Cowboy John began. "The people thought these desert animals would be good workers and pack carriers in the dry states here in the southwest."

"What happened to them?" Jimmy wanted to know.

"I'll tell you about one of them," Cowboy

John said. "Anyway, it's the way I heard it. The camel's name was Ali Abu. He came to Texas on a boat from way over in the country of Arabia."

* * * * * *

"I am called a ship of the desert, but I am certainly glad to get off that ship of the sea," Ali Abu the camel said as he stretched his legs and looked about the new country where he had landed.

For many, many days he had been strapped to the deck of the boat with other camels. There had been terrible storms on the ocean and without the straps the rough sea would have thrown the camels about and injured them. Still, it had been very uncomfortable.

When all of the camels had plodded off the boat, they kicked and ran this way and that. Strange men in plaid shirts, big hats, and boots shouted and waved ropes at them. They were so different from the other men with turbans and flowing robes that had taken care of them on the desert that Ali Abu didn't know what he was to do. Ali Abu had never seen a cowboy before.

"They shout and wave their arms," said

Ali Abu, "but no one has said 'Welcome.'"

At last the men made the camels understand that they were to go into the corral that had been built nearby. Ali Abu trotted in with the others, holding his proud head high and swinging it from side to side to look over the wide open country that was dotted with cactus and sagebrush.

"What are we going to do in this strange country?" Ali Abu's best camel friend asked.

"We are going to carry mail between the forts and take supplies across the prairie," Ali Abu replied. "I heard my master talking to the men who came to buy me."

"I don't think I will like it here," the other camel muttered.

"Hmmmm," murmured Ali Abu as he looked around for some lunch. "This looks delicious." He tasted the fence of the corral that had been built of prickly pear cactus. "Quite good," said Ali Abu to his friends. "Have a bite."

Soon all of the camels were nibbling and smacking their lips. Before long the fence was gone.

"Let's play games," Ali Abu called, and all the camels ran after him across the Texas land.

"That was fun," the camels agreed when the men had rounded them up and put them in wooden and adobe enclosures.

Many times after that Ali Abu and his friends ran away to have some fun. But it was no fun for the cowboys who had to round them up.

One day Ali Abu met some cattle going to market. The cattlemen had never seen a camel before. Two of them yelled, "Yeow! What is it?" They jumped into the river and swam to the other side and ran off.

The cattle bellowed and stamped their feet when they saw Ali Abu. They began to run.

"Stampede!" the cowboys shouted.

Ali Abu shook his head. Why did everyone get so excited? Why didn't anyone say, "Welcome, Ali Abu?"

One day a man came upon Ali Abu unexpectedly and ran off shouting, "I saw a hump-shouldered elk with no antlers."

"Hrrrumph," snorted Ali. "An elk, indeed!"

Another day Ali Abu met a farmer with a load of hay on a narrow road. The horses were as silly as the cattle and tried to turn around and run. The wagon fell into a ditch of water and made a dam. The water ran out of the ditch and into the fields and yards. The chickens flapped their wings and squawked when their feet began to get wet.

Poor Ali Abu! He was tired of eating the dry grass and shrubs that grew on the plains.

The rough stones were not like the soft sands in his own country and his feet were sore. He shivered when he heard the coyotes howl at night and he knew that they would like to have him for supper.

He seldom saw his friends any more. Some of them worked in the silver mines, others had gone with the circus, and many, like Ali Abu, roamed the prairie without a home. No cowboy wanted to ride a camel. No

rancher wanted a camel in his pasture. No cow wanted to be near them.

Finally Ali Abu went with some kind men who came for him. He found himself in a clean wire pen. All around him were other pens with animals from all over the world.

A lion roared at Ali Abu and a tiger paced back and forth and curiously watched the camel.

"Where am I?" asked Ali Abu.

"You are in a zoo," the zebra told him. "You'll like it here."

Ali Abu saw children running toward his pen and they waved and called, "Hello! Welcome, Ali Abu! Welcome to our zoo!"

Ali Abu smelled the green food in his pen and saw the fresh water. He felt the smooth ground under his feet. He liked the children's voices.

"I'm glad I've found a home," said Ali Abu with a contented sigh.

* * * * * *

"And that is what happened to the camels," said Cowboy John as he finished the story.

"I guess horses are better for cowboys, at that," Jimmy said.

IAGOO, THE INDIAN STORYTELLER

by MARGARET COMPTON

IAGOO, the storyteller of the Indians, is a little old man with a face as black as the shell of the butternut and a body like a twisted stick. His eyes are twice as large as other men's, so that when a bird flies past him he sees twice as many feathers on it, and all the little colors underneath are bright to him. His ears are twice as large as other men's, so that what seems to them but a tiny sound is to him like the roll of thunder. His legs are supple and his arms are strong, so that he can run faster and farther, and can lift and carry twice as much as others.

No one believes him, yet everyone is eager to listen to him. He tells of things of which no one else ever saw the like. But the stories are pleasant to hear, and Iagoo says they are true. When the rivers and lakes are frozen so that the Indian cannot fish, and the snow has drifted many feet in thickness so that he cannot hunt, then he goes into his wigwam, wraps himself in a bearskin

wrapper or crouches by the warm fire, and longs for Iagoo to appear. When the Storm-fool dances about the wigwam and throws the snowflakes, hard and dry as sand, in at the doorway, then Iagoo is most likely to visit him.

He vanishes for many moons and comes back with new and wonderful tales. He has met bears with eyes of fire and claws of steel, mosquitoes whose wings were large enough for a sail for his canoe, and serpents with manes like horses.

Once he found a water lily with a leaf so broad that it made a petticoat for his wife. At another time he saw a bush so large that it took him half a day to walk round it.

As he sat in his doorway one summer evening he shot an arrow without taking direct aim. It killed a swan and twenty brace of ducks that were swimming on the river, then passed on and mortally wounded two loons on the bank, bounded back and, as it touched the water, killed an enormous fish.

He remembers when the oldest oak was an acorn. He says that he will be alive long after the white man has disappeared from the land.

THE TALE OF THE STAR MAIDEN

by MARGARET COMPTON

THE Ojibways were a great nation whom the fairies loved. Their land was the home of many spirits, and as long as they lived on the shores of the great lakes the woods in that country were full of fairies. Some of them dwelt in the moss at the roots or on the trunks of trees. Others hid beneath the mushrooms and toadstools. Some changed themselves into bright-winged butterflies or tinier insects with shining wings. This they did that they might be near the children they loved and play with them where they could see and be seen.

But there were also evil spirits in the land. These burrowed in the ground, gnawed at the roots of the loveliest flowers and destroyed them. They breathed upon the corn and blighted it. They listened whenever they heard men talking and carried the news to those with whom it would make the most mischief.

It is because of these wicked fairies that the Indian must be silent in the woods and must not whisper confidences in the camp unless he is sure the spirits are fast asleep under the white blanket of the snow.

The Ojibways looked well after the interests of the good spirits. They shielded the flowers and stepped carefully aside when moss or flowers were in their path. They brushed no moss from the trees, and they never snared the sunbeams, for on them thousands of fairies came down from the sky. When the chase was over they sat in the doorways of their wigwams smoking, and as they watched the blue circles drift and fade into the darkness of the evening, they listened to the voices of the fairies and the insects' hum and the thousand tiny voices that night always brings.

One night as they were listening, they saw a bright light shining in the top of the tallest tree. It was a star, brighter than all the others, and it seemed very near the earth. When they went close to the tree, they found that it was really caught in the topmost branches.

The wise men of the tribe were summoned and for three nights they sat about the council fire, but they came to no conclusion about the beautiful star. At last one of the young warriors went to them and told them that the truth had come to him in a dream.

While asleep, the west wind had lifted the curtains of his wigwam and the light of the star fell upon him. Suddenly a beautiful maiden stood at his side. She smiled upon him, and as he gazed speechless she told him that her home was in the star and that in wandering over all the earth she had seen no land as fair as the land of the Ojibways. Its flowers, its sweet-voiced birds, its rivers, its beautiful lakes, the mountains clothed in green—these had charmed her, and she wished to be no more a wanderer. If they would welcome her, she would make her home among them, and she asked them to choose a place in which she might dwell.

The council was greatly pleased, but they could not agree upon what was best to offer the Star Maiden, so they decided to ask her to choose for herself.

She searched first among the flowers of the prairie. There she found the fairies' ring, where the little spirits danced on moonlight nights. "Here," thought she, "I will rest." But as she swung herself backward and forward on the stem of a lovely blossom, she heard a terrible noise and fled in great fear. A vast herd of buffalo came and took possession of the fairies' ring, where they rolled over one another and bellowed so they could be heard far on the trail. No gentle Star

Maiden could choose such a resting place.

She next sought the mountain rose. It was cool and pleasant, the moss was soft to her dainty feet, and she could talk to the spirits she loved, whose homes were in the stars. But the mountain was steep, and huge rocks hid from her view the nation that she loved.

She was almost in despair, when one day as she looked down from the edge of the wild rose leaf she saw a white flower with a heart of gold shining on the waters of the lake below her. As she looked, a canoe steered by the young warrior who had told her wishes to his people, shot past, and his strong, brown hand brushed the edge of the flower.

"That is the home for me," she cried, and half-skipping, half-flying down the side of the mountain, she quickly made her way to the flower and hid herself in its bosom. There she could watch the stars as well as when she looked upward from the cup of the mountain rose. There she could talk to the star spirits, for they bathed in the clear lake. And best of all, there she could watch the people whom she loved, for their canoes were always upon the water.

A STORY OF NIAGARA

by MARGARET COMPTON

BENDING Willow was the most beautiful
girl in a tribe noted for its handsome
women. She had many suitors, but she re-
fused them all, for her love was given to a
young warrior of a distant nation who, she
felt sure, would some day return to throw
a red deer at her feet in token that he wished
to marry her.

Among her suitors was an old Indian chief who was very rich. He was scarred and wrinkled and his hair was as gray as the badger that burrows in the forest. He was cruel also, for when the young men were put to torture to prove themselves worthy to be warriors, he devised tests more dreadful than any that the tribe had ever known. But the chief, who was rightly named No Heart, declared that he would marry Bending Willow, and, as he was powerful, her parents did not dare to refuse him. Bending Willow begged and pleaded in vain.

On the night before the day set for the marriage, she went into the woods, and throwing herself on the ground, sobbed as if her heart would break. All night she lay there, listening to the thunder of the great cataract of Niagara, which was but a woman's journey from the village. At last it suggested to her a sure means of escape.

Early in the morning, before anyone was stirring, she went back to her father's wigwam, took his canoe and dragged it to the edge of the river. Then stepping into it she let it adrift and it headed quickly toward the Falls. It soon reached the rapids and

97

was tossed like a withered branch on the white-crested billows. It went on and on swiftly and surely, to the edge of the great Falls.

For a moment only, she saw the bright green water, and then she felt herself lifted

and was borne on great, white wings which held her above the rocks. The water divided and she passed into a dark cave behind the rainbow.

The spirit of Cloud and Rain had gone to her rescue and had taken her into his lodge. He was a little old man, with a white face and hair and beard of soft, white mist, like that which rises day and night from the base of the Falls. The door of his lodge was the green wave of Niagara, and the walls were of gray rock studded with white stone flowers.

Cloud and Rain gave her a warm wrapper and seated her on a heap of ermine skins in a far corner of the lodge where the dampness was shut out by a magic fire. This is the fire that runs beneath the Falls, and throws its yellow-and-green flames across the water, forming a rainbow.

He brought her dainty fish to eat and delicate jelly made from mosses which only the water spirits can find or prepare.

When she was rested he told her that he knew her story, and if she would stay with him he would keep her until her ugly old suitor was dead. "A great serpent," added he, "lies beneath the village, and is even now poisoning the spring from which No Heart draws all the water that he uses, and he will soon die."

Bending Willow was grateful, and said that she would gladly remain all her life in such a beautiful home and with such a kind spirit.

Cloud and Rain smiled, but he knew the heart of a young girl would turn toward her own home when it was safe for her to return. He needed no better proof of this than the questions she asked about the serpent which caused so much sickness among her people.

"When you return," said Cloud and Rain, "persuade your people to move their camp. Let them come near me, and should the serpent dare to follow, I will defend them."

Bending Willow stayed four months with Cloud and Rain, and he taught her much magic, and showed her the herbs which would cure sickness.

One day when he came in from fishing he said to her, "No Heart is dead. This night I will throw a bridge from the foot of the waters across the Falls to the high hills. You must climb it without fear, for I will hold it firmly until you are safely on the land."

When the moon rose and lighted all the river, Cloud and Rain caused a gentle wind to raise the spray until it formed a great white arch reaching from his cave to the distant hills. He led Bending Willow to the foot of this bridge of mist and helped her to climb until she was assured of her safety and could step steadily.

All the tribe welcomed her, and none were sorry that she had not married No Heart. She told them of the good spirit, Cloud and Rain, of his wonderful lodge, of his kindness, and of the many things he had taught her.

At first they would not entertain the idea of moving their village, for there were pleasant fishing-grounds where they lived, and by the Falls none but spirits could catch the fish. But when strong men sickened and some of the children of the Chief died, they took down their lodge poles and sought the protection of the god spirit.

For a long time they lived in peace and health, but after many moons the serpent discovered their new camp and made his way there.

Cloud and Rain was soon aware of his

arrival, and was very angry because the serpent dared to come so near his lodge. He took a handful of the magic fire and molded it into thunderbolts which he hurled at the monster. The first stunned him, the second wounded him severely, and the third killed him.

Cloud and Rain told them to drag the serpent to the rapids and hurl it into the water. It took all the women of the tribe to move it, for it was longer than the flight of twenty arrows. As it tossed upon the water, it looked as though a mountain had fallen upon the waves, and it drifted but slowly to the edge of the Great Falls. There it was drawn between the rocks and became wedged so firmly that it could not be dislodged, but coiled itself as if it had lain down to sleep. Its weight was so great that it bent the rocks, and they remain curved like a drawn bow to this day. The serpent itself was gradually washed to pieces and disappeared.

In the Moon of Flowers the young warrior whom Bending Willow loved came and cast a red deer at her feet, and they were happy ever after.

HOW MAD BUFFALO FOUGHT
THE THUNDERBIRD

by MARGARET COMPTON

ONCE upon a time the Indians owned all the land around the Big Sea Water. The Good Spirit had smoked the pipe of peace at the Redstone quarry and called all the nations to him. At his command they washed the war paint from their faces, buried their clubs and tomahawks, and made themselves pipes of red sandstone like the one that he had fashioned. They, too, smoked the peace pipe, and there was no longer war among the nations, but each dwelt by its own river and hunted only the deer, the beaver, the bear, or the bison.

In those happy days there lived on that shore of the Big Sea Water, which is directly under the hunter's star, an Indian whom all his nation trusted, for there were none like him in courage, wisdom and prudence. From his early childhood they had looked to him to do some great deed.

He had often mastered the grizzly bear and the strong buffalo. Once he captured a buffalo ox so large and so strong that a dozen arrows did not kill it, and from that day he was known as Mad Buffalo.

When the magic horns were needed for medicine by the people, Mad Buffalo went forth in the Moon of Flowers and by cunning, not by magic, cut them from the head of the Great Horned Serpent. For this the people loved him and he sat with the oldest and the wisest of the tribe.

Their greatest trouble in those days was the mysterious thunderbird, which was often seen flying through the air. It had black and ragged wings, and as it moved swiftly overhead, darkened all of the earth. On moonlight nights no harm came; but when it passed in the daytime, or when the Moon-princess was journeying to see her brother, the Sun-prince, and her shining lodge was hidden by the beautiful red, the thunderbird did evil to all who fell under its shadow.

Great curiosity existed as to its nest, but no one had dared to follow it, nor had any hunter discovered a place where it seemed likely that it could hide. Some thought it lived in a hollow tree, others that its home was in the sandstone caverns, but it had never been seen to alight.

One day in the winter, Mad Buffalo set out in search of food for his family. He had to travel to the lodge of the beavers across the Big Sea Water and far up the river. He trapped a fat beaver, slung it over his shoulder and started for home just as the full moon showed through the treetops.

While crossing the lake, when he was in sight of his own wigwam, a great shadow passed before him, shutting out all light. After it had gone he looked about him for the cause. The night was clear and the moon so bright that the hunter's star could be seen only faintly, but objects about him were as plain as in the day.

At first he saw nothing, for the thunderbird was directly over his head; but as it circled he caught sight of it. It made a swift movement downward, pounced upon him and lifted him with all he had into the air.

He felt himself rising slowly till he was far above the earth, yet not so far as to prevent him from seeing what was going on below. He could even see his own wigwam and his children in the doorway. They saw him and were terribly frightened. Their mother failed to comfort them, for they knew by heart all the dreadful tales that were told of the thunderbird. They themselves had seen the beautiful birch tree which they had often climbed, torn up by the roots and left black and dead in the forest. And the oak tree where the warriors assembled was split to its base by this terrible creature. The yellow cedar whose boughs were used for the canoe that sailed on the Big Sea Water was scorched and blighted by the thunderbird.

Mad Buffalo's heart did not fail him. He grasped his spear firmly and waited his chance to do battle with the monster. Faster and faster they went toward the north, straight across the Big Sea Water, rising higher and higher in the air.

At last they came to a great mountain where no trees grew. The top was a solid, bare, rugged rock, while the sides were formed of sharp boulders, with here and there a small patch of coarse grass and a few stunted furze bushes. In a cleft of the highest rock overhanging the water was the nest of the thunderbird.

Still Mad Buffalo was not afraid. As the bird neared its home it croaked and muttered, and the sound was echoed and re-echoed till the noise was deafening. Worse than this, the creature tried to dash him against the rock, driving him toward it with its wings; and when these struck him his flesh stung and smarted as if touched by coals of fire.

By violently wrenching himself and balancing his spear, he managed to escape uninjured. At length with one powerful blow the bird drove him into its nest. It then flew away.

Mad Buffalo was stunned, but only for a moment. On coming to himself he heard a low crackling noise of thunder and found that he was left to the mercy of a brood of wild, hungry young thunders, for whose food he had probably been brought. They began at once to pick at him, uttering croaks like the old bird, only not so loud. But as there were many, the sound was, if possible, more dreadful.

Inasmuch as they were young birds, Mad Buffalo supposed they would be helpless; and when the old bird was out of sight he

dared to fight them. Raising himself as well as he could, he struck at one with his spear. Thereupon they all set upon him, beating him with their wings and blinking at him with their long, narrow, blood-red eyes, from which darted flashes of lightning that scorched his hands and face. In spite of the pain, he fought bravely.

One by one their strength failed them and they were beaten down into the nest. Mad

Buffalo took hold of the largest and strongest, wrung its neck and threw it over the precipice. On seeing this the others crept close together and did not dare to touch him again.

He seized another, killed it, threw the body away and spread the skin over the edge of the nest to dry. Then, filling his pipe from a pouch of wolf skin suspended from his belt, he sat down to smoke. Later he killed the rest of the birds and threw them into the Big Sea Water, saving only their hearts and claws.

When he had killed them all, he took four short whiffs at his pipe, pointing as he did so to the kingdoms of the four winds, asking them for assistance. Then he got inside the dry skin, fastened it around him with the claws he had saved, put the hearts of the young thunders on his spear and started to roll down the side of the mountain.

As he tumbled from rock to rock the feathers of the skin flashed like fire insects. When he was about halfway down he straightened himself out and, lifting the wings with his arms, found that he could fly. He moved slowly at first, but was soon used to the motion and went as fast as the great bird could have done.

He crossed the Big Sea Water and winged his way over the forest until he came to the place from which he had been taken ten days before. There he alighted, tore off the bird's skin and started homeward.

His wife and children could hardly believe that it was he, for they supposed the young thunders had long ago picked his bones. He broiled the hearts of the birds, which crackled and hissed so that they could be heard a mile from the wigwam, but the meat was juicy and tender.

The old bird was never seen again in that part of the country. Hunters who came from the Rocky Mountains said that it built a nest on the highest peak, where it raised another brood that sometimes came down toward the earth, despoiling the forests and the grain fields. But they flew higher than formerly, and from the day that Mad Buffalo fought them they never interfered with men.

Now, when Indian children hear the fire crackling, they say it is the hearts of the young thunders, for all their nations know of the brave deed of Mad Buffalo.

HIDDEN GOLD

by FELIX SUTTON

THE red rock walls of Devil's Gorge rose a hundred feet high on either side of the sandy canyon floor. A narrow wagon road, hardly wider than a trail, twisted its way through the litter of boulders that had toppled down from the canyon's rim.

It was a scorching afternoon in midsummer. Nevada Holden and his pal, Bill Nord, rode lazily through the gorge, holding their ponies to a slow walk to keep them from getting overheated and tired. They were going nowhere in particular, and were in no hurry to get there.

Bill shifted his weight in the saddle and wiped his face with his neckerchief.

"Wow!" he exclaimed. "I'm sure glad we got the last of those stray cattle rounded up yesterday. It's too hot to do anything today but lie in the shade." He looked around at the shimmering stone sides of the canyon. "If," he added as an afterthought, "you can find any shade."

Nevada grinned. "It's never too hot," he said, "for a boy to study his lessons. So while we're loafing along we'll have a little lesson in tracking." He pointed to the wheel marks in the road ahead. "Read that sign and tell me what you make of it."

Bill hooked his right leg across the saddle horn and bent low over his horse's withers.

"Well," he said after a few minutes, "a wagon went down this trail about two hours ago. Maybe around eleven o'clock this morning."

"How can you tell the exact time?"

"Because if it had been more than a couple of hours ago, the wind would have filled up the wheel ruts with sand. They're almost filled now, as it is."

"That's good," Nevada said approvingly. "Now what else do you read?"

"A little while after the wagon went by—not more than a half hour later—two riders followed it."

"How do you know the riders came after the wagon? Maybe they went ahead of it."

"No. The tracks of the horses' shoes overlap the tracks of the wagon wheels."

"That's fine." Nevada reached over and patted Bill on the shoulder. "You're learning fast, Billy. Anything else?"

"One of the horses was medium-size and the other was very tall. I can tell by the length of their stride. And the big horse had thrown a shoe. His left front hoof was bare."

"What color were the horses?"

Bill sat up straight in the saddle.

"Now, wait a minute," he said. "Quit foolin' me. You can't tell a horse's color from his hoof prints."

They had just rounded a turn in the canyon. Nevada stood up in his stirrups and pointed.

"No," he said, "that's so. You can't. But

there they go now. The big one is a claybank and the smaller one is a bay."

Bill looked up. Two riders were racing their ponies down the gorge, beating them sharply across the flanks with their quirts.

"They sure are in a big hurry to get out of here," he said. Then—"Hey! Look there! It's the wagon."

Nevada dug his heels into his pony's ribs. "Come on," he said. "This looks like trouble."

When they reached the battered old wagon, Bill and Nevada flung themselves off their horses. A man lay on the ground beside the wheels. He was unconscious and he had a wound on his head. The contents of the wagon were scattered all around, as though someone had been searching for something.

Nevada looked down the canyon, where the two horsemen had, by this time, disappeared.

"No use trying to catch those two now," he said. "Let's see what we can do for this old fellow."

Moistening his neckerchief with water from his canteen, Nevada began to wash the wounded man's face. He looked to be about sixty years old. He was tall and lean and thin as a rail. And his clothes were as old and decrepit as his rig. His team of two ancient sway-backed mules stood tiredly in the hot sun.

At the touch of cold water on his face, the old man groaned and opened his eyes.

"You'll never git it," he muttered, as he

tried feebly to get to his feet. "I'll never give it to ye, consarn ye! An' if I did, you'd never find it!"

Nevada held the old man in his arms and did his best to keep him quiet.

"Take it easy, old-timer," he said. "We're your friends. Try to tell us what happened."

The old prospector came at last to his senses.

"Them riders!" he cried in a cracking voice, struggling to get up. "They robbed me. They tried to make me give 'em the map. Then, when I wouldn't do it, they took it anyway."

"Now, hold your horses," Nevada said gently. "Start from the beginning. What's all this about a map?"

"The map to my gold mine. After all these years, I finally struck it rich. And now them polecats are tryin' to beat me to it."

By patient questioning, Nevada and Bill brought out the old man's story. For more than twenty years he had been prospecting the Devil's Gorge country. Only two weeks ago he had at last made his strike. But in the last town down the trail, he had talked too much. The two outlaws had overheard

him, followed him when he left town, over-
taken him on the trial, and stolen the crude
map he had made of his diggings.

"Looks like we'd better move fast," Nevada said. "Do you think you can redraw the
map from memory?"

"I sure can," the old prospector said. "I'll
never forget it as long as I live. Look here,

my name's Dode Robertson. Who are you two jaspers?"

"Folks call me Nevada. And this is my saddle pal, Bill Nord."

Old Dode's eyes widened. Then he stuck out his calloused hand.

"By cracky!" he said. "I've heard a lot about you two. I'm sure glad to have you on my side."

"All right," said Nevada, "here's what we'll do. You draw that map again, old-timer, and Bill here will ride into Cactus City with it and file your claim at the land office. If you're feeling well enough to ride one of your mules, you and I will hustle over to the mine and try to beat those claim-jumpers to it."

"You bet I feel well enough," old Dode exclaimed. He took a piece of brown wrapping paper and a pencil stub from his pocket. "Now, she lays right here, betwixt these two hills," he said. And he began to draw the map.

When he had finished, Nevada looked at the map and then handed it to Bill.

"Ride into town as fast as you can," he said, "and file this claim for Dode. Then meet us at the mine. It's likely we'll have trouble, so don't let any grass grow under your pony's feet."

Bill looked around at the land of sand-and rock.

"I'll bet there hasn't been any grass growing in Devil's Gorge for more than a million years," he said. "But don't worry. I'll fan the breeze." .

Leaping into the saddle, Bill galloped down the trail toward town.

"Come on," said Nevada to old Dode. "Let's unhitch one of these mules and get going."

Two hours later, Nevada and Dode Robertson rounded the base of a sandy hill. Dode, riding bareback on the bony mule, raised his arm and pointed.

"There she be," he said. "That's her. Over yonder below that rim-rock. There's my diggings—where you see that pile of dirt."

"The first thing we'd better do," Nevada said, "is stake out your claim and mark the boundaries. That will give you legal title to the mine as soon as Bill files your claim in town."

He stepped down from the saddle and old

Dode slid off the bony back of his mule. Carefully, the two built a mound of stones to mark each corner of the old man's claim.

Suddenly, as he was working, a bullet zinged off a rock almost at Nevada's feet. It was followed in a second by the sharp *cra-c-c-c-lc* of a pistol's report. Nevada looked up. A small cloud of black powder smoke rose from behind a huge tower of rock about fifty yards away.

"Duck, Dode!" Nevada shouted, and he threw himself behind the pile of stones that he was building. In the same motion, he drew his big Colt six-shooter from its holster at his hip. Another bullet ricocheted off the stones, making a buzzing sound like an angry bee.

Nevada caught a glimpse of a ten-gallon hat sticking up from behind the rock where the two claim-jumpers were hidden. He took a quick snap-shot with his six gun. The hat disappeared.

"Are you okay, Dode?" he yelled.

"You're darn tootin'!" came Dode's voice from behind a nearby stack of stones. "If I can get those two, this'll be the last claim they ever try to jump!"

Nevada laughed. "All right, old-timer," he said. "Save your ammunition. Don't fire 'til you see something to shoot at."

The outlaws were firing now at random. The whine of hot lead slugs filled the air, bouncing off the stones and singing away in all directions.

At that instant, Nevada saw a blur of movement from the rock where the gunmen were hidden. One of the men was trying to run to the shelter of another rock outcrop about twenty yards away, where he would have a better chance to get a shot at Nevada from the side. In a motion so fast that the eye could scarcely follow it, Nevada swung up his heavy revolver and fired. The man stumbled as though he had tripped over a hidden wire, fell forward into the sand and lay still.

"Hey! That's good shootin', pardner!" old Dode yelled. "Step over here and I'll give you your cigar."

"I'll take the cigar later," Nevada replied. "Right now I'm more interested in how I'm going to get that other bird."

He fired two more shots in the outlaw's direction to keep the man busy while he thought of a plan.

"Look, Dode," Nevada said in a loud whisper. "I'm going to circle around and get behind that fellow. You go on shooting and I'll see if I can't slip down that draw without him seeing me."

All right, pard," old Dode replied. And he let loose a barrage of shots as Nevada crawled down through the shallow draw.

Inching along, Nevada Holden circled the jagged rock behind which the outlaw was hidden. His course had taken him up the side of the hill, and when he finally got a glimpse of his man, he was about ten feet above him. The outlaw was crouched behind a projecting ledge of rock, firing at the smoke of Dode Robertson's gun.

He was dressed in a long, black frock coat and a black sombrero. The big claybank horse and the smaller bay that Nevada and Bill had seen earlier in the afternoon were standing ground-hitched behind him, their bridles dangling over their heads and dragging on the ground. The second claim-jumper still lay sprawled in the sand, where Nevada had dropped him.

Gathering his legs under him, Nevada sprang out and down.

He landed on the outlaw's shoulders and the two men went down in a heap. The bad-man's gun flew from his hand. Nevada was first to get to his feet. He swung his right fist and grazed the outlaw's jaw, knocking him back against the rock wall. The man's outstretched hand, grasping to steady himself, closed on a round piece of stone. He threw it like a baseball and struck Nevada in the forehead. Nevada slumped to the

ground, and the outlaw scrambled to find his revolver. He had just got it in his hand and was thumbing back the hammer when a loud voice said, "Okay, mister! Drop it!"

It was Bill Nord. The outlaw dropped his gun and raised both hands over his head.

Old Dode came racing across the canyon floor from his hiding place to keep the outlaw covered. Bill helped Nevada to his feet.

"Nice work, Bill," said Nevada. "It looks like you got here just in time."

Back in Cactus City, one claim-jumper was

in jail and the other one—the one Nevada had shot—was in the town's hospital. Bill, Nevada and old Dode Robertson sat in the Sheriff's office.

"Well," said the Sheriff, "you really nailed a prize pair of pigeons this time. These two men have been wanted in every state in the West. There's a $5,000 reward on their heads."

"Wow!" shouted Bill. "Split three ways, that's almost $2,000 apiece!"

"Don't count me in," said old Dode Robertson. "Getting my mine back is all the reward I want."

"Don't count me in either, Bill," said Nevada Holden. "If you hadn't come along when that fellow crowned me with a rock, I wouldn't be here to talk about it."

"Looks like that reward money is all yours, Bill," the Sheriff smiled. "It won't be long before you're old enough to go away to college, son. And that money will come in real handy."

Old Dode Robertson slapped his leg and chuckled.

"It looks like I wasn't the only one," he said, "who found hidden gold today!"

Use this easy, convenient way to build your child's library of
Read-Aloud Books

READ-ALOUD Stories About Children In Other Lands

BLACK BEAUTY TO READ ALOUD

READ-ALOUD FUNNY STORIES by Thornton W. Burgess

Favorite Poems TO READ-ALOUD

READ-ALOUD KINDERGARTEN STORIES

READ-ALOUD STORIES FROM CHILD LIFE

POLLYANNA TO READ ALOUD

READ-ALOUD ROMPER ROOM STORIES

FAIRY TALES TO READ-ALOUD

STORIES FROM JACK and JILL TO READ ALOUD

PUPPY STORIES

RAGGEDY ANN STORIES TO READ ALOUD